Cookie the Deserted Puppy

Cookie the Deserted Puppy

Holly Webb

Illustrated by Sophy Williams

SCHOLASTIC INC.

For Kitty

ISBN 978-0-545-63706-0

Text copyright © 2013 by Holly Webb
Illustrations copyright © 2013 by Sophy Williams

12 11 10 9 8 7   17 18 19/0

Printed in the U.S.A.   40
First Scholastic printing, March 2014

Chapter One

The littlest puppy whimpered quietly. The cardboard box had stopped bouncing, but nobody had come to get her out, and it was still very dark. She didn't like it. She didn't know where her mother was, and she was hungry.

She squeaked in frightened surprise as a low rumbling noise shook the box.

It seemed to be moving again, swinging and sliding across the floor. Her two brothers slammed into her, knocking her against the side of the box as the car went around a sharp corner.

The journey seemed to go on for a very long time, but she couldn't even curl up for a nap. Every time she managed to get comfortable, the box would slide around again, and they'd all be on top of one another. It was nothing like their rough-and-tumble games in the big basket at home. This hurt, and they couldn't go and snuggle up with their mother when they wanted the game to stop.

Pressed into the farthest corner, the puppy scrabbled anxiously against her brothers. They were sitting on her again! Then she realized that they'd stopped—the box wasn't sliding around anymore. Her brothers stood up cautiously. They listened, flinching a little at the creaky wheeze of the car's trunk opening. Then the box swung up into the air and was dropped with a heavy thud.

They heard footsteps, hurrying away. And then they were left alone.

"Are you ready to go, Zoe?" Aunt Jo was standing at the front door to their house, wearing her rain boots and her Redlands Animal Shelter fleece.

"Yes!" Zoe dashed down the hallway, stuffing a packet of dried apricots that Mom had found in the back of the cupboard into her lunchbox. She and Mom had both forgotten she'd need packed lunches this week, so Zoe's lunch was a little random. Still, she really liked honey sandwiches!

"Where's your big sister?" Aunt Jo asked, glancing down the hallway into the kitchen.

"She's still asleep." Zoe shook her head. "Kyra thinks I'm crazy, getting up early to come with you when I don't have to."

"Well, if you stayed at home with your sister all day, you'd just end up watching TV for all of spring break!" Mom called out. "You'll have a much better time at the shelter!"

"I heard that!" Kyra's voice floated down from upstairs. "I'm not asleep and I'm not watching TV. I'm studying! In bed! See you later, Aunt Jo. I'll come and pick Zoe up."

Kyra had finals coming up, so she was studying as hard as she could. Zoe was glad that Aunt Jo had said she could help out at the shelter — she normally only got to help out after school. It would have been boring being stuck at home with Kyra, and Mom couldn't afford to take any time off work. Sometimes when they were out of school, she got to spend the day with her friend Becca, but Becca had gone to visit her grandmother.

"Thanks for letting me come for the whole day," Zoe said to Aunt Jo as they walked to the shelter, which was about ten minutes from Zoe's house.

"That's all right!" Aunt Jo grinned at her. "I'm not going to be letting you off easy, you know. I've got a long list of jobs for you to do, starting with cleaning out the dog runs, then bathing the cats, and maybe even knitting some sweaters for the guinea pigs. . . ." She looked down at Zoe's worried face. "It's all right, I'm teasing you, Zo! There will be lots of useful stuff you can do, I promise, but it'll mostly be walking the dogs, if it's not too rainy. They don't get walked as much on the weekends, because that's when we get most of our visitors. They'll all be desperate for a good run outside."

Redlands was a small shelter, but it took in every kind of animal. The staff did their best to get all the animals new homes, but it wasn't always easy. Aunt Jo had been working there for three years now, ever since she'd gone to the shelter to get a cat and come home with Barney, her gorgeous tabby. She had been working as a receptionist at the local vet back then. That's how she knew all about Redlands. She'd ended up volunteering to help out at the shelter in her spare time. Then, when a job had come up as manager, she'd jumped at the chance. Zoe had been excited, too.

"You're so lucky, getting to be at the shelter every day, and see all the dogs." Zoe sighed. "I'm definitely going to work somewhere like Redlands when I'm older. Or maybe I'll be a vet," she added thoughtfully.

Aunt Jo smiled at her. "It's great to work at the shelter," she agreed. "But it does have its sad parts, too. Sometimes it makes me so angry the way people don't take care of their animals properly. And it isn't always the owners' fault, either. Sometimes they really love their pets, but they just can't care for them in the same way anymore. That's really heartbreaking." She sighed. "I just want to take them all home with me. But four cats is enough."

Having just Barney the tabby hadn't lasted very long. Aunt Jo was a sucker for big fluffy cats.

"Did anybody take a dog or cat home

over the weekend?" Zoe asked. She loved hearing about the new homes the animals went to. She liked to imagine herself in some of the stories Aunt Jo told. She would have loved to have a dog from the shelter, but she knew they couldn't. It wouldn't be fair to leave it all alone in their house while Mom was at work, and Kyra wasn't really a dog fan, either. She'd been chased across the park by a huge Bernese mountain dog when she was about four. She and Mom had been on their way to school, and Kyra had been on her scooter. The dog was only trying to be friendly, but Kyra hadn't known that, and she'd fallen off trying to get away from him. She'd been scared of dogs ever since.

"Edward got chosen this weekend!"
said Aunt Jo. "Finally! I'm so pleased,
Zoe. I thought he'd never find a home!"
Zoe grinned. Edward was one of the
older dogs—a bulldog. A lot of people
seemed to think that they were weird-
looking. Everyone always wanted a
cute little puppy, but Edward had
such a sweet nature.

"An elderly man came in," Aunt Jo went on. "He wanted Edward right away. He said that he'd always had bulldogs, and Edward was a great dog, and a bit of a klutz—just like him!"

Zoe giggled. "He is a little clumsy. He does bump into things."

Aunt Jo laughed. "One of the staff members did a home visit, because Mr. Johnson wanted to take Edward home with him that day. She said it looked perfect. A nice little yard, and right near a park for good walks. She said Edward and Mr. Johnson were a perfect match—both of them on the elderly side. You know Edward never liked walking very fast!"

Zoe nodded. She'd taken Edward around the park with Aunt Jo and a couple of the other dogs from the shelter before. It was the slowest walk she'd ever been on!

"Lucky Edward. And lucky Mr. Johnson," Zoe said. "I bet they're having a great time." She linked her arm through Aunt Jo's, and leaned against her with a sigh. "I know we can't, but I really wish I could have a dog of my own. . . ."

Chapter Two

The box seemed to be getting colder and colder. The April night had been freezing, and the puppies had huddled together to stay warm. They weren't used to being outside at night, and there was only the thin cardboard box between them and the concrete steps. They had always slept in their comfortable basket, snuggled up next to their mother. The cold was a frightening shock.

The smallest of the three, the tiny girl puppy, woke up first. She was miserably stiff, the cold aching inside her, and she scrabbled worriedly at the cardboard under her paws. Her two brothers were still asleep, curled up together, but somehow during the night she had rolled away from them. Now she was on her own in the corner of the box, shivering and hungry.

She tried to scratch at the side of the box, wondering if she could get out and somehow find her way back to her mother.

But even her claws hurt this morning, and she felt weak and sleepy. Too feeble to claw a hole in the side of a box.

She still didn't understand what had happened. Why had they been taken away from their mother, and their warm basket? Was someone going to come and get them, and take them back to her? When they'd been put into the box, she'd heard her mother barking and whining—she hadn't wanted them to go any more than they had. The littlest puppy had a horrible feeling that they might not be going back.

Zoe and her aunt were almost at the shelter. Zoe could feel herself speeding up. She loved it when they were the ones who opened up at Redlands — it was a real treat, and usually only happened if Aunt Jo let her come and help on a Saturday. She knew that all the animals would be excited to see them after the night on their own. The dogs would be the most obvious about it, jumping around and scrabbling at the wire mesh on the front of their pens, and barking like crazy. But even the cats, who usually liked to be more standoffish, would spring up from their baskets and come to see who was there. The shelter had a big pen full of guinea pigs at the moment, so there would be lots of squeaking from them as well.

Aunt Jo was searching in her bag for the keys, so it was Zoe who first noticed that there was something strange on the front steps.

"What's that?" she asked curiously, frowning at what looked like a box in front of the main door to the shelter.

Aunt Jo looked up from the bunch of keys. "What?"

"There. On the steps. Maybe someone's donated food to the shelter, Aunt Jo!" People did bring in pet food for the animals occasionally—Zoe had seen them. "It's funny that they didn't bring it in when there was someone who could say thank you, though."

"Mmmm . . ." Aunt Jo was walking faster now, the keys dangling forgotten in her hand.

22

"What's the matter?" Zoe asked. She could see that her aunt looked worried.

"People leave us other things, too, Zoe," Aunt Jo sighed. "It might be an abandoned animal in that box. If it is, I suppose that at least they've brought it to us, but I hate it when they just leave it like that."

Zoe felt her eyes filling with tears. The box was just a box, a shabby cardboard one. How could someone stuff a cat or a dog in there, and then just leave it? It was so mean!

They hurried up the steps and sat down slowly, one on either side of the lid. Aunt Jo took a deep breath. "I never get used to this," she murmured as she started to unfold the flaps on the top. "It's been such a cold night. Look, there's frost on the top. If there's something inside, I hope it hasn't been in there long."

There was a feeble scrabbling noise from inside the box, and Zoe caught her breath. "There is something inside there!"

Aunt Jo frowned at the box. "Yes.

And I'm being silly, Zo. We should take the box inside. We don't want whoever's in here getting scared and leaping out."

Zoe nodded. "Good idea. Can I take it?" she asked hopefully. "You unlock the door."

Carefully, Zoe slipped her hands underneath the box, shivering as she touched the clammy, cold cardboard. Whoever was in it must have spent a miserably cold night. She heaved the box up, and felt something inside it wriggle.

There was a worried little squeak, and a yap.

"It's okay," she whispered. "We're just taking you into the shelter. It'll be nice and warm in there. Well, warmer than out here, anyway."

Aunt Jo had unlocked the doors now, and she was turning off the alarm. She held the door open for Zoe, and they hurried into the reception area, putting the box down on one of the chairs.

"I think it's a dog," Zoe told her aunt. "I definitely heard a yapping noise. But it can't be a very big dog—the box was so light."

"Let's see." Aunt Jo lifted the flaps of the box—it was supposed to hold packets of chocolate chip cookies,

Zoe noticed—and they both peered in.
Staring anxiously up at them were
three tiny brown-and-white puppies.

Chapter Three

The littlest puppy flinched back against the side of the box. She was still so tired from being bounced and shaken around, and now the light was flooding in, after hours of being shut in the dark. It hurt her eyes and she whimpered unhappily. Her bigger, stronger brothers recovered more quickly, bouncing up to see what was happening, and where they were. But the little girl puppy pressed her nose into the corner of the box, hiding away from the light. She was too cold and tired to get up, anyway.

Zoe and her aunt gazed inside, and Zoe grabbed Aunt Jo's hand. She'd never seen such little puppies at the shelter, she was sure. They were the smallest puppies she'd ever seen anywhere. "Oh, my goodness, three of them," murmured Aunt Jo.

"They're so tiny," Zoe whispered. "They barely weigh anything at all."

Aunt Jo nodded. "They're way too young to be away from their mother. They must be only a few weeks old. Good job staying quiet. We don't want to scare them.

They may not be used to seeing different people."

The puppies were looking up at Zoe and Aunt Jo uncertainly. One of the boy puppies scrabbled hopefully at the side of the box, clearly wanting to be lifted out.

"Well, he's not shy." Aunt Jo laughed quietly.

Very gently, she slipped her hands into the box and lifted out the puppy. He wagged his stubby little tail and licked her fingers. "Yes, you're a darling, aren't you?" She turned to Zoe.

"They must be starving if they've been in this box all night. Now that I'm looking at him more closely, I don't think this little boy can be more than four weeks old. He's probably only just been weaned from his mother. They should be having four or five meals a day, and a little of their mom's milk still."

Zoe giggled. "That's why he's trying to eat your fingers. . . ." Then she looked down worriedly into the box. "Aunt Jo, what about the little puppy in the corner? Is she okay? She isn't moving like the other two."

Her aunt sighed. "No, she isn't . . . We'd better take a closer look at her. Can you bring the box along to one of the puppy pens? Then we'll have somewhere cozy for them to curl up, and we can mix up some puppy milk. Maybe a little cereal mixed in it, too. We'll have to see what they think. They may not have had any solid food yet."

Zoe gently lifted up the box, with two puppies still in it, and followed her aunt through to the main shelter area, where all the pens were. Dogs jumped up excitedly as they went past, barking for their breakfast, and for someone to come and play with them. Zoe looked down worriedly at the two puppies in the box. The bigger one—she was pretty sure it was another boy—was now standing up, balancing carefully on plump little paws, and listening to the new and exciting noises. He looked up curiously at Zoe—the only person he could see at the moment.

Maybe he thinks it's me barking! Zoe thought to herself, smiling down at him.

But her smile faded as she looked over to his litter mate. The tiny puppy was still curled miserably in the corner of the box. She didn't seem to want to get up and see what was going on at all.

"We'll put them in here—nice and close to the kitchen," Aunt Jo said, opening one of the pen doors and crooning to the puppy snuggled in the crook of her arm. "I'm pretty sure we've got some of that powdered puppy milk replacement left," Aunt Jo murmured. "And some of the made-up bottles. I'd better order some more, though."

She sat down on the floor in the pen

with the puppy in her arms, and Zoe put the box down next to her, kneeling beside it. "Should we take the others out?" she asked, looking at the boy puppy, who was clawing excitedly at the side of the box now.

Aunt Jo nodded. "Be careful though, Zoe. Don't scare them. They might not be very big, but puppies can still nip if they're frightened. Get the bigger puppy out first, then we can let him explore with this one, while we see what's the matter with the tiny one."

Zoe reached in and picked up the puppy, who was still standing up against the side of the box. He wriggled and yapped excitedly, and when she put him down on her lap, he squirmed around eagerly, trying to see everything in the pen. Then he nuzzled Zoe's fingers and wriggled carefully down the leg of her jeans, heading for the floor. He obviously just wanted to explore this new place.

The other boy puppy was still snuggled on Aunt Jo's lap, looking around curiously, but not quite confident enough to go marching around like his brother.

"Try just petting the little one very gently," Aunt Jo advised. "Don't pick her up right away. She isn't looking at us, and she'd get scared."

Zoe reached in and ran one finger down the puppy's silky back. The brown fur was so soft, but she didn't feel as warm as her brother. "She's pretty cold," Zoe said, glancing around at Aunt Jo. "Even just touching her. And she's sort of floppy."

Aunt Jo bit her lip. "She's suffered more being out all night because she's smaller. Here, put this on your lap, Zoe." She lifted a soft fleece blanket out of a padded basket in the corner of the pen. "Then lift her out carefully and wrap her up. Just loosely. And keep your hands around her to warm her up a little."

Zoe nodded, and gently cupped one hand around the puppy. The tiny dog shivered a little as she felt Zoe's fingers, and turned her head slightly. But she was just too weak to look up. Zoe slipped the other hand underneath her, and lifted her out onto the blanket. She wrapped it around the puppy, petting her gently through the folds.

"Okay, little one," Aunt Jo murmured to the puppy on her lap. "I need to go and get your sister a hot-water bottle. And make up some milk for you guys. Hmm? Want to go and see this nice basket?" She lifted the puppy into the basket, and petted him for a few seconds until he got used to being somewhere new. Then she got up slowly. The other boy puppy trotted over to the basket, too, nosing affectionately at his brother.

"Those two seem fine," she said, sounding relieved. "And I'm sure they'll be even perkier once they've had something to eat."

Zoe looked up at her. "What about this one?" Her voice wobbled. "You don't think she's going to be all right?"

Aunt Jo sighed. "We don't know yet. She seems very weak. I'm going to call Sam at the vet's and ask if she'll come over as soon as she can to take a look at them. Are you okay with them for a minute, while I get a hot-water bottle for the little one?"

Zoe nodded, still gently rubbing the puppy through the blanket. She wished she could feel her moving. The puppy felt like a saggy little beanbag, slumped on her lap. Carefully, she moved the blanket from around the puppy's head, peering down at her. Her eyes were closed, and her pink tongue was sticking out of her mouth slightly. It looked dry, Zoe thought worriedly. Aunt Jo had better hurry up with that puppy milk. She hoped they'd be able to persuade the puppy to drink it. She didn't look like she wanted to make the effort to do anything right at the moment.

"Here's the hot-water bottle," Aunt Jo said, hurrying back. "I've wrapped it up so it isn't too hot."

"Do we put her on top of it?" Zoe asked, starting to lift the puppy off her lap.

"No, that would be too hot. I'm going to put it at the side of the basket, then she can snuggle next to it. We'll just have to keep an eye on her brothers, and make sure they don't nudge her away."

"Maybe we ought to put her in a pen on her own," Zoe said doubtfully. "They're a lot bigger than she is. They might push her around."

"I'd rather keep them together if

we can. She's already lost her mother, and her home. Her brothers are the only security she knows. Also, if we separate her, she might find it difficult to manage being around other dogs when she's bigger."

Zoe nodded as she laid the puppy close to the hot-water bottle. "We don't want her to be lonely," she agreed.

"I've started to warm up some puppy milk. I'll go and get it, and we can see what they think." Aunt Jo went into the kitchen, and came back with a shallow metal tray of the special puppy milk. "Hopefully, they won't tip this over," she explained to Zoe, who was looking at the tray in surprise—it looked like something her mom would make chocolate brownies in.

The two boy puppies had been nosing around the edges of the pen, trying to explore, but as soon as Aunt Jo put the tray down, they galloped over to see what it was—so fast that they got tangled up and fell over each other. They struggled up to their feet, mock-growling, and then scurried up to the tray, sniffing at it excitedly. It only took seconds before they were eagerly drinking, burying their tiny muzzles in the milk and splashing it around.

"They must have had milk from bowls before," Zoe said, watching them and giggling.

"Maybe. Or else they're just fast learners," said Aunt Jo. "I don't think we need to worry about them not eating. I'll mix a little cereal into the next batch." But she was frowning. "I'd really hoped that the smell would wake the little one up, but she doesn't seem to have noticed. We'll have to try feeding it to her with a bottle."

Zoe nodded. "Should I put her on my lap?" she asked hopefully. She'd loved holding the puppy before, and trying to warm her up. Even though it was frightening that the puppy was ill, it felt really special to be the ones trying to make her better.

"Yes. Unwrap her, and we'll try to get her to take a bottle. I brought one just in case." Aunt Jo took a baby's bottle with a cap out of the pocket of her fleece, and sat down next to Zoe. "She's still so sleepy. . . ."

The puppy was really floppy now, and she didn't wriggle when Zoe unwrapped her. Aunt Jo held the bottle up to the puppy's mouth, but she didn't seem to notice it. She certainly didn't start sucking, as Zoe had hoped she would. She only turned her head away a little, as though Aunt Jo nudging the bottle against her mouth was annoying.

"She doesn't want it," Zoe said worriedly. "Is there anything else we can give her?"

"We could try using a syringe. . . ." Aunt Jo said thoughtfully. "We can poke it into the corner of her mouth, and try and trickle it in." But Zoe could see that her aunt was doubtful about the puppy ever feeding at all.

"What about . . ." Zoe brushed her fingers against the tip of the bottle, letting a few drops of milk ooze out of the tiny hole onto her fingers. It was thick and yellowish, not like ordinary milk at all. Holding her breath, she stroked her milky fingers across the puppy's mouth, letting the milk run onto the dry pink tongue.

The puppy shivered with surprise, and the little tongue darted out, licking Zoe's fingers.

"She likes it!" Zoe squeaked.

Aunt Jo smiled. "Quick, you take the bottle. Squeeze a little out onto the tip, and dribble it into her mouth."

The puppy licked eagerly at the bottle this time, and when Zoe pushed it gently against her mouth, she sucked, harder and harder, until she was slurping messily at the milk.

And then, at last, she opened her dark eyes and stared up at Zoe.

Chapter Four

To: Becca
From: Zoe
Subject: Puppies

Hi Becca!

Hope you're having a good time at your grandma's. Sorry I haven't emailed you for a couple of days. Been sooooo busy! I went to the shelter with Aunt Jo on Monday, and someone had abandoned three puppies in a box on the front steps!!! (Here's a photo.

Aunt Jo took it on her phone. Aren't they cute?) It was a box that was supposed to be for chocolate chip cookies, so we've named the two boys Choc and Chip, and the little girl puppy Cookie. She's really sweet. When we first found them she was really weak and Aunt Jo told me afterward she wasn't sure she was going to make it. We're giving her milk from a bottle because she won't eat mashed-up cereal, even though her two brothers love it! (You should see them eating—it goes everywhere, and we have to wash them afterward!) But some of it must be going inside them—they're getting fatter every day! Cookie is definitely getting bigger, too, and she likes me to carry her everywhere! I've got lots more photos that Mom's printed out for me. I'll show you when you get back.

Love, Zoe xxxxxxxxxxxxx

Hi Zoe!

I can't believe you found puppies! You are so lucky. Grandma's is okay but it's a little cold at the beach. I went wading and my toes almost fell off.

Will the puppies get new owners from the shelter? How old are they? I wish I could come and see them. Guess what? Mom and Dad say we can definitely get a dog (you know they wouldn't make up their minds before). But now they say we have to go slow and make sure we find the right dog! Aaargh! I really want to have a dog NOW! Please ask your aunt if I can come and see the puppies when I get back. Maybe one of them could be our dog!!!

From Becca xxxxxxxxxxx

Zoe read Becca's reply to her email, smiling to herself. Becca wrote emails just like she talked. But her smile faded a little as she read on to the end. Becca was so lucky to be getting a dog. Zoe had been talking to Aunt Jo about the puppies today at the shelter. They'd been weighing them to check that they were eating enough, which was difficult because Choc, Chip, and Cookie saw no reason why they should stand still on top of the scales, and just kept bouncing around. In the end, Aunt Jo had made a guess at their weights, but she said they were definitely getting heavier, which was the main thing.

Then they'd taken five minutes just to play with the puppies—it seemed

like fun, rather than work, but Zoe
knew it was actually really important.
If the puppies didn't get played with,
they wouldn't know how to behave
with their new owners.

"How could anyone have abandoned them?" Zoe asked sadly, watching Chip and Choc dashing up and down the pen, chasing after a ball. Cookie was scampering after them, not quite brave enough or fast enough to take the ball from her brothers, but having just as much fun. "They're so beautiful, all of them. How could anyone be so mean?"

Aunt Jo sighed. "Well, at least they brought them here. It was a start."

"But they left them out in the cold all night!"

"Some people just don't think. The puppies were probably an accident — they hadn't had the mom spayed, and then maybe the owners felt they couldn't afford to buy all the puppy food, and take the puppies to the vet for vaccinations. Dogs are expensive to look after." She reached over to put her arm around Zoe's shoulders. "Don't think about it, Zo. The puppies were lucky they ended up here, so they've got all of us taking care of them. We're going to turn them into sweet, well-behaved dogs, and make sure they only go to great owners. They won't remember any of this."

"I hope not," Zoe whispered with a tiny sigh. Aunt Jo's words were supposed to make her feel better. She knew the puppies would need to leave the shelter in a few weeks, but she'd been trying not to think about it too much. She'd only known them for a few days, but they were so sweet,

Cookie especially. If they could stay at the shelter for a little longer, she'd be able to keep taking care of them. . . . But that wasn't fair. They needed real homes.

Reading the exciting news in Becca's email had made her think about having to say good-bye to the puppies all over again. . . .

To: Becca
From: Zoe
Subject: Re: Puppies

Hi Becca,

Aunt Jo thinks the puppies were about four weeks old when we found them, so now they're five weeks. They can't go to new homes until they're about eight weeks old. I'm sure you can come and see them. I'll ask Aunt Jo. You're so lucky to be getting a dog!

I hope your mom and dad pick one soon.

See you back at school in a week!

Love, Zoe xx

It wasn't as friendly as her emails to Becca usually were, but Zoe was feeling sad. She stared at her computer screen, not really seeing the cute photo of Cookie that she had set as her wallpaper.

"What's up?"

Zoe jumped. She hadn't heard Mom come in at all. "Nothing . . . I was just thinking about the puppies. I'm going to miss them so much when they get new homes." She gulped. "Especially Cookie."

Mom nodded. "She is beautiful." Zoe had shown Mom the puppies one afternoon at the shelter, when Mom had come to pick her up. "I think it's her eyes. She's got such a little face, it makes her eyes look huge, and then she's got those whiskery eyebrows. Has Aunt Jo figured out what breed they are yet?"

Zoe giggled and shook her head. "Nope. Everyone at Redlands thinks they're something different. Aunt Jo thinks maybe there's some Jack Russell in them and maybe some cockapoo, too. But we might not be able to tell until they're bigger. Almost grown-up. And we won't see them then, will we? So we'll never know." She sniffed, and Mom hugged her.

"But you knew they'd have to go to new homes, Zo! All the animals at the shelter do. You've never gotten this upset before."

"I know. Maybe it was because we found them—and feeding Cookie with the bottle has made her special to me, Mom." Zoe smiled proudly. "I got her to take some puppy mix and milk in a bowl this morning. Aunt Jo was really happy. She said that she'd thought Cookie was going to have to drink from bottles forever!"

"Your Aunt Jo ought to be paying you, with all the work you're doing!" Mom sighed. "I know you love it at the shelter, but maybe you should take a couple of days off from helping out. Do something else? I bet Kyra could take some time away from studying to take you shopping. Or to the movies?"

Zoe looked horrified. "Oh, no, Mom! I have to keep going. I have to help Cookie start eating solid food. It's really important."

Her mom gave her a worried look. "Well, I suppose so. . . ."

Chapter Five

"It sounds like the best spring break ever!" Becca sighed enviously.

Zoe smiled at her as they walked into their classroom. "It was great. I really missed going to the shelter this morning. I was looking forward to seeing you, but besides that, I didn't want to come back to school!"

"Me, either, but I can't see my mom

letting me take the day off because I need to go and visit the world's cutest puppies. . . ." Becca flopped down into her chair and glanced over at the board. "Math problems! Didn't miss those during break." She got out her math book, but went on talking in a whisper. "So is Cookie eating real puppy food now?"

Zoe nodded. "Yup. They all still drink a little milk, but they've started drinking water, too. And Cookie's really catching up to Chip and Choc. I don't think she'll ever be as big as they are, but she's doing okay. I brought the photos Mom printed out. I'll show you later—Shh!—Mrs. Allan's watching us right now." She stopped talking and tried to look like she was concentrating on the problems that Mrs. Allan had put on the board for them. Their teacher was usually nice, but she always got stricter when they came back after vacation—as if she thought they needed to remember what school was like!

Zoe showed the photos to Becca and some of the other girls in her class at recess, and everyone said how cute the puppies were. Lots of the girls said they were going to ask their moms and dads if they could visit the shelter and see the puppies, and maybe even adopt one of them. Zoe knew that most of her friends wouldn't be allowed to—Lucy already had two dogs at home! But the more people who came to see the puppies, the better. No matter how much Zoe hated the thought of them leaving the shelter, she wanted them to have the perfect homes.

Aunt Jo had arranged to pick up Zoe from school that afternoon for a visit to the shelter. Mom was going to pick her up after she finished work. Zoe got changed quickly in the bathroom—Mom hated her getting her school uniform dirty—and then ran to see Cookie and the others.

Cookie was curled up in their basket, watching her brothers playing tug-of-war with a bit of old rope that someone had given them. They'd had it since that morning, and it was their new favorite toy. Bits of it were scattered all over the pen. She sighed a little, and rested her nose on her paws, wondering where Zoe was. Zoe had played with her every day since they'd come here from their old home. Actually, the little puppy couldn't remember much of where they'd lived before they'd been at the shelter. The only thing she was sure of was that their mother had been at the old place. She still wondered what had happened, and why they had been taken away, but she didn't mind, because now she had Zoe.

Except that today she didn't, and she didn't understand why. Zoe always fed her and her brothers. Zoe made a special fuss over them, even though she wasn't feeding them milk on her lap anymore. Zoe still brought the food bowls, and watched to make sure that Cookie was eating well. Zoe even stopped Choc and Chip from trying to take her food if they finished theirs first.

Today, the other lady had brought their food—Jo, the one who was always with Zoe. Jo had said nice things, and she'd petted her and said how good she was. But it wasn't the same.

Cookie's little ears pricked up sharply.

Someone was running along the passage between the pens— someone with small, light footsteps. She jumped up in the basket and barked excitedly as Zoe appeared at the front of the pen, beaming at her.

"Oh! Did you miss me? I really missed you," Zoe told her, opening the latch. "You, too, yes, I missed you, too, you great big monsters," she told Chip and Choc, patting them lovingly as they waltzed around her feet. But it was Cookie that she sat down next to, and Cookie she cuddled as soon as the puppy clambered happily into her lap.

"I missed you more," Zoe whispered

into her ears as she petted her. "I know I shouldn't really say it, but I did." She sighed. "There's some people coming to visit, Cookie. Try and look like a perfect pet, okay? You aren't old enough to get adopted for a couple more weeks, but if they like you, they might wait."

She could hear them coming along the line of pens. A couple who'd just bought a house together, and were thinking of getting a dog. They'd said they didn't mind whether it was a puppy or an older dog, but when Aunt Jo had mentioned the three gorgeous little puppies, they'd gotten excited.

"They'll want to meet you." Zoe sighed again. "They looked nice, I guess.

Nice-ish . . ." She couldn't imagine anyone being a good enough owner for her sweet Cookie. No one except her, she realized, with a miserable little gulp.

"So they decided on Jasper?" Zoe asked as she helped her aunt clean out the food bowls, feeling a bit surprised, but very relieved. Jasper was about five years old and was a mixed-breed, mostly Labrador. He wasn't nearly as nice looking as Cookie and her brothers, Zoe thought.

"Yes, they decided that they wanted a bigger dog after all," Aunt Jo explained. "Don't worry, Zoe. It won't be hard to find homes for those three at all. They're beautiful. It's the older dogs that it can be hard to place."

Zoe nodded. "My friend Becca is going to get a dog soon. Becca said she'd love to come and see the puppies. She's going to ask her mom and dad if they could come this weekend. That would be okay, wouldn't it?" Her voice wobbled a little. "It'll only be one more week till the puppies are old enough to go to new homes. . . ."

Aunt Jo looked closely at her. "Yes, they'll be about seven weeks this weekend, as far as we can tell. It won't hurt them to be split up from their litter after eight weeks. It would be lovely for one of your friends to come. Zoe, are you okay, sweetheart?"

"I'll miss them, that's all," Zoe muttered.

"I know you will. Especially Cookie. You've looked after her so well. But she can't stay here, Zo, you know that. It isn't a good life for a dog, in a little pen like this, however much we love them."

"I know. But it's hard to think of someone else taking her home. I wish we could have a dog! I'd take really good care of her!" Zoe burst out. Then she added quietly, "Don't worry, I know we can't. . . ."

Aunt Jo hugged her, accidentally clanging two stainless steel dishes together behind her back, and making Zoe laugh.

"I'm so excited!" Becca raced up the steps toward Zoe, her mom following behind her. She flung her arms around Zoe. "Please can we see *all* the dogs? And the cats? I know we don't want a cat, but I'd like to see them, anyway. And the guinea pigs!"

"I'll show you everything," Zoe promised, giggling. She hadn't seen her friend so hyper since her birthday party. She took them all around the shelter, saving the dog pens for last.

"You're so lucky, getting to help here all the time," Becca told her, cooing at the guinea pigs. Then she looked excitedly up at her mom. "Please can you show us the dogs now, Zoe? Mom and Dad said we might be able to get one really soon. That's what Dad's doing today—fixing our fence so that there aren't any holes at the bottom, and it's safe for a dog to be in the yard. He said if we found a dog from somewhere like here, the shelter would want to come and check that we'd take good care of it."

Zoe nodded. "Yes, Aunt Jo and the other staff members go and look around everyone's houses. They wouldn't let you have a cat from here if you lived on a really busy road. Or if you had little kids. You'll be all right," she added. "You want a dog and it's only *really* little kids that are a problem—you know, too little to understand about not pulling tails."

Becca nodded.

"Doesn't your dad want to help choose a dog?" Zoe asked curiously.

Becca's mom smiled. "This is just a first look—so we can think about what sort of dog we'd like. Becca's dad will come and see them if we tell him there's a dog we really like. But he started worrying about the fence last night, and he was determined to get it done. He didn't want us to miss out on a great dog because the house wasn't ready."

Zoe smiled. It sounded as though Becca and her mom and dad were really serious about getting a dog. They weren't just deciding to adopt one without thinking it through, like some people did. "Okay, look, well, here are the dog pens. It can get a little noisy!" she warned Becca as several of the dogs started to bark excitedly when they realized they had visitors.

"Oh, look . . ." Becca whispered,

glancing from side to side. "So many! Freddie . . . oh, Luca—he's so cute, Mom, look! He looks like a German shepherd. Oooh! Trixie!" Becca crouched down by the little spaniel's pen. "She's so pretty. . . ."

She glanced up worriedly at Zoe. "How do people choose? She's looking at me, like she really wants us to take her home, and I haven't even seen half of the pens yet!"

"It is hard," Zoe admitted. "If you think you really like any of the dogs, tell me, and I'll ask Aunt Jo if you can go into the pen and meet them."

"If I did that, I'd never be able to say no," Becca's mom muttered. "What if we cuddled a dog and then said we didn't want him? It would be heartbreaking!"

Zoe wrinkled her nose. She supposed she was more used to the shelter than most people. "I know it's sad. But Aunt Jo and the others do find homes for all the dogs in the end. It can take a while for some of them, though." She led Becca and her mom along the row of pens. "And these"—she stopped by a pen—"are the puppies we found abandoned." She laughed as all three of them raced toward the wire of the pen. "The one with the darker brown patches is Choc, and that one's Chip. . . ." She pointed to the puppy with the brown eyepatch. "And this one, with the pale brown patches"— she paused—"is Cookie."

"Oh, wow . . ." Becca murmured. "They're all so beautiful!"

"They are lovely," her mom agreed. "They look very little, Zoe. Are they old enough to be adopted?"

"Not for about another week," Zoe explained. "But then it will be fine, although they still can't go outside for a while after that. All the dogs in here have been vaccinated, but puppies have to have a last set of vaccinations when they're about twelve weeks old. Then they can go for walks. They'd be okay in the yard, though," she added.

"You know a lot about dogs," Becca said admiringly. "Please, can we meet them? Mom, do you want to?"

Her mom nodded, smiling. "Definitely."

Zoe swallowed hard, and opened the latch on the pen. It was good that Becca and her mom liked the puppies. But it was one step closer to them leaving the shelter, and Zoe.

Cookie scrabbled excitedly at the wire. Zoe had been playing with them earlier, and then she'd disappeared. Now she was back!

But there were other people, too. Another girl, like Zoe, and someone else. Cookie had never seen them before. She stopped wagging her tail quite so hard, and backed up a bit as Zoe opened the door. She wasn't used to different people.

Zoe let Becca and her mom in, and Chip and Choc sniffed cautiously at them. Becca picked up the last bit of the rope toy and whisked it along the ground, right in front of Choc, who quickly pounced on it, pretending to growl.

"He's so funny!" Becca giggled.

"I think he's the friendliest of the puppies," Zoe told her. She looked around for Cookie, who was almost hiding behind her, watching Becca and her mom with big, anxious eyes. "It's all right, Cookie," she whispered.

Cookie pressed herself against Zoe's side and sniffed cautiously at Becca's mom's fingers when she held them out. The new people smelled nice, but she didn't know them like she knew Zoe. She didn't mind if this lady petted her, though.

"She's very sweet," Becca's mom said. "Is this the one you bottle-fed, Zoe? You can see that she adores you."

Zoe smiled sadly. She loved it that Cookie acted like her dog, even though she wasn't. She sighed. Cookie was going to have to learn to love someone else. Gently, she lifted Cookie up and put her on Becca's mom's lap.

Cookie froze and sat motionless, her shoulders all hunched up under her ears. She looked around worriedly at Zoe, but she didn't wriggle off. It was all right. Zoe was still there, very close. The lady petted her ears, which was nice. She relaxed a little, and licked her hand.

"She's a little bit shy, but she's very loving," Zoe said, trying not to mind that someone else was cuddling Cookie. She took a deep breath. "She'd be a wonderful pet. Any of them would."

Cookie watched sadly, her ears flattening back, as they all got up. They were going, she could tell. She missed Zoe so much now that she didn't stay all day, the way she used to. Zoe had been here longer today, but Cookie still hadn't had her lunch. Cookie liked it when Zoe brought her food and sat with her while she ate. She always ate more when Zoe was there, because Zoe liked to see her eat, and she would tell her what a good dog she was, eating so well.

As Zoe was shutting the front of the pen, Cookie raced after her, scrabbling her claws against the wire netting and whining sadly.

"It's okay," Zoe whispered to her. "I'll be back tomorrow. I promise."

Cookie didn't know what that meant, but she understood Zoe's comforting voice. She stopped whining and just stood up against the wire, staring after the girls as they walked down the passageway between the pens. She watched until the doors swung shut and she couldn't see Zoe anymore. Then she dropped down and sadly padded over to their basket, her claws clicking against the worn tile floor.

Chapter Six

"Mom says we can have pancakes for lunch," Becca told Zoe happily as they took their coats off.

"I love pancakes," Zoe said, trying to sound a bit more cheerful than she felt. It was a treat to go to Becca's house, but she would have preferred to stay at the shelter with Cookie and the others for a little longer. It would be rude to say that, though.

The girls curled up on the sofa and watched a movie. Zoe was careful not to let herself think about how nice it would be if there were a little puppy snuggled up between them, watching, too. But then, next time there might be. Becca's dad was still outside fixing the fence. When they'd gotten back, he'd shown them the shiny new wire running neatly around the base of the old wooden fence. They'd taken a cup of tea out to him, and a plate of cookies, and he'd said gratefully that he thought he was nearly finished. It looked like their whole family was really committed to having a dog.

Becca had gone to get them both some juice, leaving Zoe watching the movie—they'd both seen it before—

and now she came running back in.

"Zoe! I've just been talking to Mom and Dad, and guess what!"

Zoe blinked at her in surprise.

"We're going to ask your aunt if we can reserve one of the three puppies! Mom's calling her now! She's arranging for them to come and do a home visit, too!" Becca was dancing around the room in delight, and Zoe stared at her.

This was good news. One of the puppies was going to have a great home, and be well taken care of. Zoe would even be able to keep on seeing whichever puppy they chose. She'd know what the puppies would look like when they were grown-up after all!

But what if they choose Cookie? the voice inside Zoe's head niggled. Then Cookie would belong to someone else. She stopped herself. This was her best friend, Becca, they were talking about. Cookie would have a great home.

"That's wonderful," she told Becca finally, swallowing back the lump in her throat. "Aunt Jo will be really happy."

"Oh, and Mom says lunch is ready," Becca added.

Zoe nodded. That was good. After lunch it would be time for her to go home, and she wouldn't have to go on trying to be happy for Becca. She knew that she ought to be, but she wasn't.

She was burningly, horribly jealous instead, and she felt terrible about it.

"We went out yesterday to that big pet shop over by the supermarket. Have you ever been there?"

Zoe shook her head.

"I hadn't, either. It's enormous, and it sells everything! You'd love it, Zoe," Becca burbled happily. "Your aunt emailed Mom a long list of stuff we'll need, and we even got some things that weren't on the list, just because they were so cute! Lots of toys! The puppies loved playing with those toys they had in their pen at the shelter, didn't they?"

Zoe nodded. "Yes," she murmured quietly, burying her head as she got her pencil case and book out of her bag.

"And we have to make sure that our puppy has lots to do, because it might be lonely without any others to play with. Although I'll be there, of course. Zoe, are you okay?" Becca added. "You're really quiet."

"I'm fine." Zoe tried to sound enthusiastic. "Did you get a rope toy? They really like that old piece of rope they've got."

"Yes! A beautiful one. Much nicer than that ratty old piece they have now."

Zoe sniffed, trying not to cry. *But they like that ratty old bit of rope,* she thought to herself. *And what if Becca chooses Cookie?* Zoe stopped herself. Whichever puppy Becca chose was going to be so lucky.

I'd be a good owner, too, she said to herself miserably. *I know so much about looking after dogs. I've fed those puppies, and cleaned up after them, and washed them when they got themselves covered in food. . . .*

"Did you hear me, Zoe?" Becca nudged her gently, and Zoe jumped.

"Um, no. Sorry. What?"

"I just said that we're going to go to the shelter on Saturday, and choose the puppy, and then it can come home with us!"

"Oh!" So soon! Zoe swallowed hard. "That's great," she muttered. "Um, I really need the bathroom. Tell Mrs. Allan, if she comes, okay?"

Zoe tried as hard as she could to be her usual self with Becca that week, but it was so, so difficult.

Becca clearly knew that something was wrong—she wasn't stupid. Zoe kept avoiding her, and running off to return her library book instead of chatting with Becca and their other friends at lunchtime. She spent the whole of one morning recess hiding in the girls' bathroom after Becca started telling her about the pretty collars she'd seen on a pet website. They had little pawprint designs woven on them, and space for a phone number, so that if the dog got lost it was easy for someone to call you. It had just made Zoe feel too upset. When the bell rang, she'd had to tell Becca she felt sick.

Zoe hated lying to her friend all the time, but she didn't want to admit how jealous and sad she was really feeling.

By Friday, Becca had stopped telling her about all the things they were doing to get ready for the puppy. She almost wasn't talking to Zoe at all. And at lunch Becca went off and played tag with a group of other girls in their class, without even asking Zoe if she wanted to join in.

"See you tomorrow morning," she told Zoe rather awkwardly, as they got their coats on at the end of the day.

Zoe nodded. "Yes. Bye, Becca."

And that was that. No running out to the gate together. No promises to call later about homework. Becca just walked away, leaving Zoe fiddling with the zipper on her jacket and feeling completely miserable.

Kyra was waiting for her outside school as usual—the high school was just up the road from Zoe's school. She usually got out later than Zoe did, but Zoe had taken forever that afternoon.

"Are you all right?" Kyra asked. "You look really sad."

Zoe shrugged. "I'm sort of not talking to Becca," she admitted. "It's horrible."

"Did you have a fight?" her sister asked sympathetically.

"No." Zoe sighed. "It's all my fault. You know the puppies at the shelter?"

Kyra laughed. "No, Zoe, it's not as if you've ever talked about them at home."

Zoe swung her schoolbag at her sister, making a face. But Kyra was always good at cheering her up. "She's going to adopt one."

Kyra smiled, and then looked confused. "But that's good, isn't it?"

"Yes," Zoe said in a small voice. "I just wish I could, too, that's all. I'm jealous. . . . And worse than that, I'm worried that she might choose Cookie."

"Oh, Zo . . ." Kyra hugged her. "Look, I haven't met these puppies, but I can see how much they mean to you. Why don't we visit the shelter, so you can show them to me?"

"But you hate dogs!" Zoe stared at her.

"I don't hate them." Kyra shrugged. "I think I'm getting better. One of my friends at school has a really cute spaniel. I even let him sit on my lap on the couch the other day."

"Wow, Kyra! That's great!" Zoe smiled. "Of course I'll show you the puppies. You're going to love them, 'specially Cookie—she's really cute—I was going to ask Mom if she could take me over there later, but let's go now." She grabbed Kyra's hand and practically dragged her down the road.

"All right, all right, don't pull my arm off!" Kyra grinned.

It didn't take them long to walk across the park toward Redlands, and soon they were turning into the driveway.

"I brought Kyra to see the puppies!" Zoe told Aunt Jo as they popped their heads around the office door.

Aunt Jo looked up from her computer. "Hi, Kyra!" She grinned. "That's great news."

"Hi, Aunt Jo." Kyra smiled back. "I just thought I'd like to see them. Mom said they were really cute."

"They are." Aunt Jo nodded. "I'll call your mom and tell her you're both here. I can take you home in the car if you like."

"That would be great," said Zoe. "Come on, Kyra—they're down here." Zoe grabbed Kyra's hand and pulled her down the hallway. "Don't worry. I don't think there are any really big dogs in the shelter at the moment," she added, seeing her sister glancing cautiously into the pens.

"I just don't like it when they jump against the wire," Kyra murmured.

"Chip and Choc do jump up, but they're really little," Zoe promised. "Cookie won't, not till she's figured out who you are. She's a little shy."

"Okay. Oh, Zoe, are these them?" Kyra stopped in front of the puppies' pen, smiling at them. They were all asleep, for once, flopped in a sort of puppy pile in their basket. The pile heaved and wriggled every so often, and as Zoe gently undid the front of the pen, it struggled apart and turned into three hairy, whiskery brown-and-white puppies who frisked happily around Zoe's feet.

"Do you want me to bring one of the puppies out?" Zoe asked. "Then you could pet just one—you wouldn't have them jumping about."

Kyra nodded, and Zoe picked up Cookie. Cookie nuzzled at her happily. She'd been hoping that Zoe would come soon. She looked around curiously as Zoe carried her out of the pen, leaving her two brothers behind, looking rather jealous. Cookie stared down at them, wagging her stubby little tail.

Zoe was carrying her to another girl, a taller girl with the same dark hair and eyes. Cookie looked at her with her head to one side—the girl looked a lot like Zoe. But she didn't seem to be confident with dogs the way Zoe was. She looked kind of nervous and, as she put out her hand, she patted her very quickly, as if she thought Cookie might snap.

Curious about this girl who looked so much like her favorite person, Cookie wriggled in Zoe's arms, stretching toward the other girl.

"She likes you!" Zoe said laughing.

"She does?" Kyra asked, sounding surprised and pleased.

"Yes, she does," said Zoe. "Do you want to hold her?"

"I don't know. . . ." Kyra looked uncertain. "Okay, let me try." Kyra nodded slowly, then let Zoe put Cookie into her arms.

Cookie snuggled up against Kyra's chin, and slowly, Kyra petted her ears. The little dog closed her eyes.

"Oh, Zoe, she's adorable." Kyra smiled down at the puppy. "No wonder you've been spending so much time here."

"She is, isn't she?" Zoe sighed sadly. "And now I just can't bear to think of letting her go. . . ."

Chapter Seven

Cookie scampered down the outdoor yard, chasing after the jingly ball. It was her favorite toy. She loved the noise it made, even though she didn't quite understand where the noise came from. It was definitely hers—Zoe had given it to her. It was the only toy she bothered to fight over.

Chip raced past her and dived onto

the ball, rolling over with it in his paws, growling excitedly.

Cookie let out a sharp, furious bark and jumped on top of him, scrabbling to get the ball back. Unfortunately, Chip was still quite a bit bigger than she was, and he wriggled and growled. Then somehow he was sitting on top of her instead, and he still had the ball, in his teeth now. He shook it backward and forward, still growling, so that it jingled madly.

"Stop fighting, you two!" Zoe ran over. "Chip, Chip, look! Your bone! Your best bone! Come on! Where's it going?"

Chip sprang up, dropping the ball and dancing around in circles as Zoe waved the blue rubber bone. Then she flung it away, and he galloped after it like a racehorse.

Cookie seized her ball gratefully and sat down on Zoe's feet, panting.

"You really love that, don't you?" Zoe reached down and picked her up. "Look, there's a nice sunny patch there. Let's just sit and watch those two brothers of yours being silly. . . ."

It was a beautiful warm May day, and Zoe had shorts on for the first time that year. She should have been feeling happy, but all she could think about was Becca. She'd be here soon. Which puppy would she choose? Zoe ran her hand gently down Cookie's back, over and over, as Cookie shook the ball gently to and fro, listening to the jingly noises.

"What if she chooses you, Cookie?"
Zoe whispered. "I've been trying not to
think about it. It was bad enough just
thinking about Becca having a dog, and
me not being able to have one. But what
if it's you that she wants to take home
with her?" She sighed and leaned over,

resting her cheek against Cookie's wiry fur for a moment. "I guess at least I'd still get to see you. That's if Becca ever talks to me again, the way I've been this week. I've been awful."

Cookie looked around at her for a moment, her eyes dark and sparkly. She licked Zoe's hand.

"Thank you!" Zoe grinned. "Was that to tell me you don't think I've been awful? I have, though. I was horrible, actually. I just can't tell if it would be worse to never see you again, or to see you belong to someone else! I don't know whether to hope that Becca chooses you or that she doesn't." This time Zoe heaved a massive sigh so that Cookie turned around and stared at her. "Sorry! Did I shake you up and down?"

"Zoe!" Aunt Jo was calling her. "Becca and her mom and dad are here! They're just getting out of their car. Go and say hello. I'll bring these three in."

"Oh! Okay." Zoe gently put Cookie down, and the puppy scampered off after the ball again. She walked slowly through the shelter to the reception area, where Becca and her parents were now talking to Susie, who was at the reception desk.

"You two can chat while we fill these out," Becca's mom told them, smiling.

Becca must not have told her mom how grumpy Zoe had been all week, Zoe realized gratefully. "Hi . . ." she said to Becca.

"Hi." Becca stared at her, and then

she pulled Zoe over into the corner, as if they were going to look at photos on the wall of the dogs and cats who'd been adopted recently. "Zoe, is there something going on?" she asked. "Are you mad at me?"

Zoe turned red and looked at her feet. "No . . . I . . . ." She didn't know what to say.

"You are!" Becca cried out. "You've been acting really weird all week! What it it? What have I done?"

Zoe sighed. "Nothing. Nothing at all. I know I've been weird, but it isn't your fault. It's me. I've been jealous . . . jealous because you're getting a dog, and I can't have one, not ever. We don't have anyone at home to take care of a dog during the day, and Kyra hates them, anyway. I'm so sorry I've been horrible."

"Oh, Zoe." Becca gave her friend a big hug. "Why didn't you tell me?" she asked her, stepping back, her eyes round with surprise. "I'd have understood!"

"I guess I just felt stupid. And mean," Zoe muttered. "And I didn't really want to talk to you about it. You were so excited. . . ."

Becca sighed. "I didn't think about it making you sad," she admitted. "Did I go on and on about it?"

108

Zoe gave a very small giggle. "Yes. All the time."

A voice behind them interrupted the awkward moment. It was Becca's dad. "Are you girls ready?" he asked them. "I want to see these wonderful puppies you've been telling me about!"

Becca looked anxiously at Zoe, but Zoe nodded, managing to smile and look almost as though she meant it. "Come on!"

They walked down the passage to the puppies' pen. Zoe spotted Aunt Jo coming back in from the yard with the puppies in her arms. "There they are," she told Becca's dad, pointing. "They've been playing outside."

The puppies saw them, too, and started to wriggle excitedly. Aunt Jo laughed and crouched down, letting them run down the passage toward the visitors.

Cookie dashed ahead, streaking toward Zoe on her tiny little legs. Zoe was desperate to pick her up and cuddle her. But she couldn't. It was Becca's turn.

But Becca wasn't looking at Cookie, Zoe realized. She'd crouched down and was holding out her arms. Chip was running straight up to her, and now he was standing on his hind legs, his front paws on her arms, giving happy, excited little barks. He licked her cheek and jumped, as though she was the best thing he'd ever seen!

"He remembers me!" Becca cried delightedly. "I've only met him once, but he really remembers me! Oh, Dad, do you like him? His name is Chip. He's the cutest of all of them. Please, can he be ours?"

Chapter Eight

Zoe watched, smiling, as Becca hugged Chip. He wriggled delightedly in her arms. So it would be a stranger who would be taking Cookie home, she realized sadly. She wouldn't see her adorable little puppy grow up into a beautiful dog after all.

Cookie patted her paws hopefully at Zoe's leg, asking to be picked up.

She could tell that Zoe was sad, but Cookie knew that she could make her feel better. When Zoe lifted her up at last, Cookie stood up in her arms, rubbing her whiskery nose against Zoe's cheek. That always made her laugh.

"You're so sweet," Zoe murmured, but she didn't sound much happier.

Cookie watched interestedly as the girl cuddling Chip gave him some crunchy treats and carefully lifted him into a sort of box, like a small pen with a wire front. She shivered a little, burying her nose in Zoe's neck. It reminded her of the box they'd all been shut up in. It felt like a very long time ago now.

Chip looked confused, and whined, but the girl fed him some more treats through the wire, and then the man with her picked up the box, and carried him away down the passage to the door.

Cookie gave a little whimper of surprise. They could go away? Chip was going with that girl, and the other two people? She didn't understand. If they were allowed out of the shelter, why didn't Zoe take her when she went? Maybe she would! Maybe they were all going! Cookie's tail started to flick back and forth with excitement.

"Well, that was good, wasn't it?" Aunt Jo said, sounding really happy. "And I meant to tell you, Zoe, a really nice-sounding family called me asking about puppies, and they were interested in getting a boy puppy—so that would be you, Choc." She looked down at the puppy in her arms, who'd barked when he heard his name. "Yes, you! They're going to come and see you tomorrow, aren't they, sweetie? So we're getting there."

Zoe nodded. That would leave just Cookie. And she wouldn't be there for much longer, either, Zoe was sure.

"Oh, look, there's your mom and Kyra," Aunt Jo pointed out, and she turned to open the front of the pen and put Choc back in.

Zoe sighed and walked toward the pen to put Cookie in, too. She'd forgotten that Mom was coming to pick her up early. She wanted them to go and do some shopping—Zoe needed new school shoes. Zoe had told Mom that she could just buy them for her, but Mom had said no.

Cookie twisted in her arms, struggling frantically and whining. She wasn't going back in the pen— she wanted to stay with Zoe! Someone had already taken Chip away. Only Zoe could take her.

"What's the matter?" Zoe gasped, holding the puppy tightly and backing away from the pen, as that seemed to be what was upsetting her.

"Is Cookie okay?" Mom asked worriedly. She and Kyra had just come into the passage between the pens, and now she was hurrying toward Zoe.

"She got really upset when I was trying to put her back in the pen." Zoe cuddled Cookie close against her shoulder. She could feel the little dog's sides heaving, she was shaking so badly. "Maybe she's sad about Chip going?" She wrinkled up her brow. "It's okay, Cookie. It's okay," she whispered. But then her eyes filled with tears. "I'm telling her everything's going to be all right, but it isn't," she said miserably, looking between Aunt Jo and Mom. "Chip's gone to a new home, and Choc will probably go, too, tomorrow, and then it'll be just Cookie left. And someone will choose her really soon, and we'll never see her again."

Aunt Jo frowned. "I wonder if she does know what's happening. Some dogs really do seem to understand a lot more than you'd think they could. Maybe that's why she doesn't want to go back into that pen."

"But she has to," Zoe said dismally. "What are we going to do? Do you think she'd be better if we moved her into a different pen?"

Aunt Jo glanced at Mom, and shook her head. "No, to be honest, I think it would just be better if she went home with you."

"But then it would just be harder for her to come back." Zoe blinked, not really understanding what her aunt was saying.

"Or we could keep her," her mom said, putting an arm around Zoe's shoulders and gently patting Cookie.

Zoe looked puzzled. "But there's no one to take care of her in the daytime."

Her mom glanced at Aunt Jo. "We've been talking about that. I told your aunt I was worried about how much you were falling in love with Cookie. That you were going to be really upset when she went to her new home."

"And I said you were so good with dogs, you really deserved to have one of your own," said Aunt Jo.

"So we've come up with a plan," said her mom.

"I'm going to have her here at work with me in the day, Zoe," Aunt Jo explained. "She can have a basket under my desk, and I'll take her for a walk at lunchtime."

"And Kyra?" said Zoe, flashing her sister a look.

"I don't feel scared of Cookie," said Kyra. "She's a little sweetheart. Mom told me how much you'd bonded with Cookie—it was actually my idea we should adopt her. That's why I wanted to meet her last week."

"Really?" Zoe stared at them all, her eyes like saucers. "You mean it? We can have Cookie? So—so we could take her home now?" Zoe whispered, hardly daring to hope that they'd say yes.

Aunt Jo smiled. "Well, she obviously doesn't want to go back in that pen. I can stay here and make a big fuss over poor old Choc, so he doesn't mind being on his own. And you can borrow some food bowls and things, until you can get your own."

Zoe nodded, thinking how much allowance money she had saved up, and how she was going to spend all of it at the pet shop on the little puppy. Cookie was going to have the nicest things she could find.

"You're coming home with us," she

whispered to Cookie. "You really are."

Cookie nudged Zoe's cheek with her damp black nose, and looked hopefully at the door.

"Look at them! They're having such a good time," Zoe said. She laughed at the two little brown-and-white dogs — Chip and Cookie. Who would have thought it? They were standing at the bottom of a huge tree, right at the ends of their leashes. And they were both jumping up and down, barking themselves silly.

"I wonder if Choc likes chasing squirrels, too?" Becca said to Zoe thoughtfully. "Maybe we'll see him in the park one of these days."

Zoe nodded. "I bet he does. And I bet he never catches them, either."

The squirrel was sitting high up in the tree now, looking down at the two dogs in disgust. They hadn't come anywhere near him, and he clearly wasn't very worried. He almost looked like he was yawning.

Eventually, Cookie and Chip gave up on the squirrel and wandered back to Zoe and Becca.

"Cookie's catching up to him," Becca commented. "She's almost as big as he is now. She might even end up being bigger!"

"Maybe," Zoe agreed. "They probably won't finish growing until they're about nine months. Maybe even a year. They're four months old now, so they've got five months more growing to do, at least. You're going to be a huge dog one day, aren't you?" she told Cookie affectionately, crouching down and ruffling her ears and petting her back.

Becca giggled. Cookie might get bigger one day, but she and Chip were still tiny at the moment. Not that they seemed to think they were little at all. They strutted through the park as if they thought they were the most important dogs there.

"They wouldn't fit in that box now," Zoe said suddenly, looking up at Becca.

Becca shook her head. "I still don't know how someone could have left them like that. But I'm glad it was you and your aunt Jo who found them."

Zoe nodded, scratching Cookie under the chin, so that she closed her eyes blissfully and her tail thumped on the ground.

"I know. Me, too."